Gurley Street Love

Loving You the Gurley Street Way

D. Othniel Forte
Berenice A. Mulbah

Forte Publishing

Monrovia. Bangkok. Virginia.

First Published in 2020 Published by:

FORTE Publications
#12 Ashmun Street
Snapper Hill, Monrovia, Liberia
[+231] 777155-923
[+231] 881-106-177

FORTE Publishing
7202 Tavenner Lane
208 Alexandria
VA, 22306

FORTE Press
76 Sarasit Road, Ban Pong, 70110
Ratchaburi, Thailand
[+66] 85-824-4382

http://fortepublishing.wix.com/fppp
fortepublishing@gmaill.com

Printed in the United States of America

ISBN:
ISBN-13: 978-0-9935710-9-1

Curley Street, a Red-light district in Monrovia

Contents

Authors' Note

Sex isn't always the most comfortable topic in our society, at least that is what they'd want us to believe. The reality is, we are confronted with it every day. We do not believe it is a taboo. Direct, frank and candid discussions around or about it is the taboo. But in truth, sex is an integral part of our society.

It is not easy to dispel a belief or unlearn some things, however, neither is it impossible.

Our candidness and perhaps kinky approach to sex is unusual. It may even be an affront to some, we are not ignorant of that, but we make no apology either. Though we may not wish to offend any, we fully accept that some might be. We only hope that, with time, we can find a common position to agree upon.

Of the many abled writers to do this book, we strongly believe that no one else was better suited, than this duo, to write it the way it is done. This is important because we wanted it to be done exactly like this. We wanted a harsh, raw, up-in-your-face approach to getting out our message.

We've been asked, if we were not afraid of what this could do to 'our reputitions' or how some might 'view us' after this. Some, in good faith, suggested we used pennames. But we were most clear about this. If this message was going to effect the kind of change we needed it to do, we had to be the faces behind it. On that, we never once, flinched, never disagreed, never doubted.

Now, we'd say this one last time, do not read this book if you are fainted hearted or not open to sexual explorations. Don't say you were not warned. Beyond here, is a world for the brave, adventurous and bold.

GO HAVE SOME FUN! OH, AND TELL US ABOUT IT!!.

Prologue

Sunset Monrovia

He ran out of the water, grabbed me by the waist, and pulled me closer for a kiss. Our tongues locked together, swirling, saliva, wine and remnants of roasted fish. His right hand groped my left breast whilst his left felt for my butts/ass- and rubbed it. I ran my fingers through his wet, ruffled hair and down to his cheeks. As the kiss intensified, his stiff manhood pressed against me, firing me up. The sudden touch of his icy cold fingers between my thighs- its coldness against my warmth- sent a shiver up my spine.

"Ooh," I sighed and tightened my grip careless I might choke him.

He fumbled with my thin swimsuit, looking for an entrance to my vagina. When they entered the murkiness of my wetness, I exploded with passion.

1

Endless Love

The Bliss

Lover's Beach

On the far side of a private beach, a couple was silhouetted just enough to see that they were making out. Not that it was a big deal but it was arousing the few within view of them.

On the far side of the beach

"Oh no, oh no, oh no," I screamed, trying to hold myself back from coming. My left hand covered my eyes, while my right hand tried pushing his head away from between my legs. They were shivering, my legs of course.

His tongue made its way into corners of my pussy, first the clitoris, then the mouth before scaling the walls. It roamed, licking every inch.

He finally lifted his head after a good minute of digging into me. Those pink lips of his glossed with my pussy juices.

"Hmm, dam it jue, you are sweet like hell. No, you swee pah palm wine. I swear to Gor, my geh, dah one der, no joking busney insah. My hay jeh spinning."

I smiled with satisfaction as I pulled him up, over my chest. His body rested on my double D's soft but firm breasts. I reached for his lips. They were wet and juicy. Then, he gave me his tongue and straight into my mouth, I took it.

I couldn't help but think, "Mehn, the boy can work magic with his tongue." In no time, my pussy started watering up again. I sucked on his tongue harder. He slowly elevated his body, just enough to get his hand rightly positioned for the touch. The strong, long fingers on his other hand fondled my pussy.

His large, wet, other hand grasped my breast and caressed them like they were all that mattered to him. Oh my! My body started to let go, losing control, as my juices began running like Kpatawe waterfall. I felt my legs closing up, with him in the middle. I wanted it, I had to have it, but more so, I needed his dick deep inside me immediately.

"Oh my God, please, please, put it in," I begged.

His left hand let go of my breast and made its way up to my neck. Impatient, I groped for him in the dark. I fumbled a bit but I got it. Using my hand to guide it, I shoved it inside my vagina. It entered the murky soup with a slurp sound.

"Hallelujah, hallelujah," my pussy walls started singing. "Oh my goodness, oh my goodness." It felt good, it felt so dam good. His dick was the perfect fit.

"Sweet Jesus, this *man* was everything I had always imagined he would be; everything I wanted. He has just confirmed that he was all that and more.

Tall, check.

Dark, check.

Handsome, √check.

Educated, √check.

Gentle, √check.

Financially stable, √check.

Funny, √check.

Spiritual, √check.

Physically fit, √check.

Moreover, boy, the dick is on point, double check √ √.

Now that I had gotten him, I did not intend to let him out of my grips, not ever!

****

Those Daydreams

Tamba was my boss' son and my colleague. He was smart, dam good at his job and had great looks.

His body though... Hmmm, that was another thing. He kept his body fit. It was always shining as if he had robbed oil on it. It reminded me of newly molded milk candy. It was just perfect.

He wore a smile that melted my heart. At the office, he has this thing he does every time he stops by my desk to greet me. He'd make a smacking sound.

When he does that, my heart just beats like *1-3-5-7* instead of *lub-dub, lub-dub*.

Whenever we are in a meeting, he walks in with an air of command and takes charge like, "I was born for this." His words fall off his lips with ease. Everything about him is just smooth.

However, he doesn't know that I feel this way about him. It's all in my head. Often, I sit there daydreaming that one day, he would pick me up, place me on the table, slowly ease his way up my skirt, rip off me panties and fuck me for hours.

However, that was not *ever* going to happen. At least not in this life, because, he was way too caught up in the drama of Queta, his girlfriend and soon to be wife, to even consider the idea. So, I was just left to daydream of him. I took one solace though, "Experience player can't fight for jersey." I strongly believed that, "What was for you, shall see your face"; it was just a matter of time. And when mine comes, I'd get my due; be it him or another. Until then, I intended to enjoy my fantasy.

Interestingly, after a year of daydreaming, hugging, kissing and sucking him in my secret world, my time still hadn't come. I wondered often these days, when my time would ever come. But more importantly, what the hell was I waiting for to realize that I was fucking daydreaming over a man another woman was royally fucking. Reality needed to set in and wake me the fuck up or I might just die and have burgorbor eat my fat, wasted pork.

Tamba wanted to be just like his father, so he studied hard and became a lawyer. His father's firm hired him and he worked with his dad as junior partner. For years, he learned everything there was to know about the business, plenty about the law and got just the right connections and clients. He worked hard for this position.

I joined the law firm just about three years ago. I was a young lawyer without any experience, but his dad took a chance. I've worked so hard to prove to him that he hadn't made a mistake by hiring me. So far, the Old Boy seems pleased with my work, he has given me more responsibilities, and taught me a lot.

The moment I met Tamba, it was an instant connection. We laughed and talked about what life was like as law students. We joked about how nervous we were in the courtroom on our first cases. Eventually, we started to talk about more than just work.

He told me much about his beautiful girlfriend, how they grew up together. Her family knew his family and they were planning to get married. It was a beautiful love story. I must admit, sometimes, I was jealous.

I felt she was not the one, but that was not my place to tell him. Of course, that didn't stop me from wanting to tell him so.

She had no interest in his job; they couldn't even keep a long conversation. She was too busy being chasing those designer clothes and looking pretty, to have interest in anything more than the next big thing in fashion.

But, I guess she was giving him some good pussy otherwise, he would not be caught up in her charm. I mean, the brother could not see past that girl.

Over time, I learned to ignore her and focus on our friendship. We often worked late, so he ended up taking me home several times. We even got to making time so we could 'consult' on important cases.

On one of those rare occasions when I actually left the office before nine, I heard the knock at my door. This was strange because I don't entertain guests, more so past that ungodly hour. I am normally in bed by then. "Who is it?" I asked.

"Fine girl, come open the door, it's Tamba."

"Tamba? What are you doing here," I asked as I ran in my room to put on some clothes. I had just walked out of the shower and was about to get in bed butt naked as usual.

"If you open the door, I will tell you what I am doing here."

"One minute please."

I couldn't find anything but my lappa, which was on the bed. I quickly picked it up and wrapped it around my body.

I rushed to the door, heart racing and all, opened it and there he was, a body of pure muscles. I could see he had been working out a lot lately, because his lean arms had turned into arms of a gym rat, if you know what I mean, muscles popping everywhere. He just had to come to my house wearing a sleeveless shirt too. "If only he knew the dirty thoughts, I had playing in my mind, he would not try me," I thought.

He rushed past me, into my living room.

"Is everything ok?"

"Everything is more than ok."

"Let me guess, you guys settled on a date?"

"No, even better."

"Then, what?"

"I just got off the phone with my dad; he is turning the firm over to me." His father needed to rest, so he turned over the family business to him. It was something he had wanted all his life.

"Oh my god, no way. Oh my god, this is good, this is really good."

"I know, I know," he said, doing a 360-cartwheel dance.

Then it occurred to me, "Wait a minute, why are you here? You should be celebrating with your girlfriend."

His facial expression quickly changed. All that joy instantly turned into sadness. He walked to the sofa and took a seat. I walked after him and sat next to him.

"It's over."

"What's over?"

"Satta and I."

"What do you mean, it's over."

"We broke up."

"How? When? Why? What are you talking about?"

"We broke up about three months ago."

"Three months?"

"Yep."

"Oh hell no." I thought. I wanted to slap him. "You are telling me, I could have made a move on him three months ago and he is just telling me?" I felt upset, then stupid.

"And you never told me? I thought we were friends?"

He turned facing me and held my hands, "I was embarrassed."

"Embarrassed about what?"

"I'm not sure. I just felt stupid."

"So, what happened, why did you guys break up?"

"She broke up with me."

"She broke up with you? That's crazy. Why?"

"She said I was boring."

"Hahaha," I laughed, "you boring? That's silly."

"Yep. She said that all I wanted to talk about was my stupid job. Can you believe that, she called my job stupid?"

"Hahaha," we both started to laugh.

Then the room went really silent. I guess he was thinking what I was thinking.

He leaned over as if to kiss me, but then, he pulled back. So, I leaned into him and placed my lips on his. I started to suck his lips. They were soft. He slowly slipped his tongue into my mouth. "Mehn, it was long, perfect length for my pussy," I thought.

Suddenly, he picked me up and sat me on his lap, facing him. He opened the nose of my lappa, letting it fall. He started caressing my breast. "Mehn, you have no idea how many times I have dreamt of holding these in my hands," he said.

"What!" I thought but I didn't say anything. I was a little surprised, because every man I know wants to touch my breast. He, however, never showed any signs of wanting to fuck me, for the last three years we've worked together. So yeah, I was not expecting it because all he ever talked about was his silly coconut brain girlfriend. Well, her loss, my gain.

I leaned into his body and started licking his neck, as I rubbed my hands up and down his strong arms. I closed my eyes and took a deep breath, then I whisper in his ears, "You have no idea how many times I've come thinking about you fucking me."

From the kick of his dick hitting my butt, I knew my words had turned him on more. He quickly placed me on the sofa and stood up. His dick was hard pressed against his pants. He hurriedly pulled down his pants and there it was, in all of its glory.

I took to a knee to pay my respect. Mehn, inches, long long, big with perfectly spear like head. It was beautiful. I put it in my mouth, closed my eyes and allowed it to full mouth. I kept it there for a moment before....

The dick went deep, hitting my throat. I could see heaven gates open. My time had arrived. The good girl won, after all. Just as I had dreamt many times, a mouthful of dick. Now I had it all to myself all night long.

He froze, it seems. I felt it trying to throb up and down but there was no space so I opened my mouth and it went loose.

I sucked it slowly at first. Soon, he began moaning. His hand found my hair and gripped it tightly as he forced it back and forth. I found it difficult to breath but

I was glad to see how he was gyrating and shaking as if the Holy Spirit had suddenly descended on him. He struggled to keep on his feet as his legs fumbled about and he uttered vulgar wars. Just as I was about to stop, he exploded an avalanche of hot, acidic semen in my mouth.

2

Sweet Chocolate

Walnut, Cream and Chocolate

Monrovia was hot and we had had a messy week so, we planned a getaway. Initially, we considered Marshall City, but later settled for Bomi Hills then Cape Mount to see the Blue Lake. It wasn't too far with paved roads.

We loaded the jeep with food and drinks in a sizable cooler. Satisfied I had left nothing behind I waited for him. He entered the car and handed me a peeled off bar of cold chocolate- the dark, rich brown one. It was just how I liked it.

"Thank you darling."

"Oh so because I gave you chocolate, I am darling?"

"Just hush it. You Liberian men never know when to just take a compliment."

"Compliment, are you sure? From a Liberian woman, hmmm. Who if you told her she looks nice today, then she starts a fight, 'so dah only today I fine ehn'. I beg you yah."

"It is called gratitude."

"Gratitude my foot, that sounded more like a bribe. You Liberian women mostly, will only act nice when you receive a present."

"But seriously, when best does one show appreciation? Is it not after something has been given him or her?"

We remained joking this way until I had gone halfway through the bar, then I remembered to share with him. I reached over and put the bar in his mouth. He bit off a chunk but a piece fell on his pants. Without thinking about it, I reached for it with my mouth. As it settled on my tongue, a thought hit me. "Why don't I give him a head?"

So, immediately, I reached in his pants and pulled out his cock. It was still lamely wiggling whichever way I dictated.

He startled, "What... you know I'm driv..."

I dropped a piece of chocolate then quickly bit off a mouthful of chocolate. I crunched it into smaller pieces and allowed it to melt just enough to be milky, and then I placed his penis in my mouth.

He moaned, "Dam gal," as he stiffened his legs and arched his head against the seat.

By now, my other hand had reached for his balls and was rubbing them steadily but not hard. He opened his legs wider to make room for my head and to make himself more comfortable.

"Shit, this is good."

I paid him no mind; I just continued slurping the brown murky mixture on his walnut brown nut. Up and down, I moved my head and after several strokes, I'd stroke his cock. I enjoy how he hardened whenever I put my lips around him.

"Oh baby, yes."

I stroked faster and moaned, "Hmmm."

"Oh yes, fuck."

"Hmmm."

"Oh yeah, baby."

After we had built a rhythm, I abruptly stopped, lifted my head to observe his expression.

"No gal, don't stop, not now."

"You like it?"

"Hell yes."

"You want it?"

"Yeeessss!"

"Then beg for it!"

"Please."

"I can't hear you."

"Please baby."

"Please what?"

"Suck me." He reached for my head and tried forcing it down toward his cock which was by now fully erected, all six inches of it. I tugged at it small and put it in my mouth but not before taking another bite of chocolate. This time, the chunks had not melted so they felt like tiny pieces of ice on his cock. Each up and down movement elicited passionate melodies from him.

I stroked, sucked, squeezed gently on his nutsbag, at regular intervals, and then I suddenly stopped just when he was gyrating like some extraterrestrial being had taken over his body. I then took the head of his dick and bit it a pinch. That did it for him because he jerked so hard, I nearly hit my head on the steering wheel. When he settled down I repeated the bite-pinch.

"Fuck! You're good."

"Uhmm, was all I could manage between sucks." His dick had filled my mouth until there was no space for the chocolate. I increased the tempo of my movements as he continued jerking crazily.

He shouted countless dirty words, which turned me on but also fueled my passion.

"Open that pussy let me fuck you."

I just kept squeezing his balls, this time a bit harder. I'd squeeze, suck and bite while he yelled.

"Fucking shit!"

Squeeze.

Suck.

Bite.

"Faster baby. Don't stop. Squeeze it. Suck me gal like only you can. Oh yes, oh yes, go on. Faster and faster. Suck it until I come. Yes. Yeeeeessss. Uuuugggggghhh."

The dude was on fire. Every bone in him was shaking along with my movement. He kept going up and down in a thrusting motion. I quickly put my index finger in my mouth and lubricated it, then in one swift motion, I reached for his balls and squeezed them just hard enough to increase his tempo. Then I moved down to his ass and gently placed the wet finger at the entrance. He grabbed my head with a bundle of hair, his squeeze was so hard, it felt as if he was ripping it off my skull. He stopped moving, froze in time but for his fingers folding on my hair.

With even gentler pushes, I inserted my finger a little deeper in his ass. By now, I had him dancing to two rhythms, the head and the finger.

"Oh, God, oh God, you're killing me. What do you want to do to me ehn? I'm coming, it's coming. Suck it! Don't freaking stop! Yes, its coming! Yes baby. It's c-o-m-i-n-ggg!"

With that, he flooded my mouth with his creamy wine. The first bout went directly down my throat. I pulled back slightly to catch the rest but he held me down in that position.

When he was done, I allowed the sperm to roll down his up-righted dick. It was as thick as condensed milk. It looked so beautiful against the chocolate and walnut brown. A sparkle of ivory on dark mahogany. I admired it for a while before swooping it all up and swallowing.

I recalled my last thought being, "The power of chocolate."

The Road Trip To Nowhere

He tenderly lifted my head from his lap and placed me into a sitting position. Then, he pulled his pants up. The whole thing was messed up from chocolate mixed drippings.

It had slipped my mind that he was in a white pant. I just wanted to give my man a good time, and that I did. Tacked in well, he looked at me and said, "Dam, gal, you're the freaking best. That head was..."

I was like, "Duh."

"I swear you shook my brains."

"You better remember that whenever you are tempted to do something dumb. Ain't nowhere you'd get it this good. But if you mess with me, you're out. O-U-T! No second chances. It is all yours for the taking, any time, any way you wish, but if you slip up, I'm gone."

"That's just cold!"

"Straight talk can hurt feelings."

"Hmmm."

"'Hmmm' all you want, but that is the brutal truth. I give it one way only."

"Hey dear, no need to go all gangster on me. I'm just trying to enjoy my shid here. Could you do your mood killing talk some other time and place?"

"Whatever."

We paused briefly. Each of us going into our reveries. It was written all over his face, that head was the only thing on his mind. The glances he threw my way often, only to smile and shake his head, confirmed it. I pretended I was engrossed in my own thoughts, but I saw him out of the corner of my eye.

Oh and I, I was thinking, thinking about that monstrous cock and how it could fill my nunu up and satisfy me. I was seconds away from pulling it out and riding it, but I knew better than to mess with a dick in a moving car. Shits like that get you killed. I settled for us riding in silence. I will have my chance, when we reach our destination.

The countryside was lush, green and dam beautiful. The road was shitty in several parts; some of which were just unavoidable. Every time he bounced, my stomach churned and I felt light headed. I guess it was because I was getting close to my menses and I was stressing over how much action I'd get before that happens. I was praying for some miracle to hold it long enough until our trip was over. I'd hate myself if

I missed this opportunity. I needed to screw this guy out of his brains.

Since we began dating, this was our first time getting groovy. We'd smooched a few times but nothing this serious. I needed to be on top of my game. I could not let him walk away from here feeling regular. I planned to fuck him as he has never been humped before.

When we reached, I went straight for the shower. I was so engrossed in the hot water, I didn't hear him enter behind me. I only felt his hand on my arm. I startled and tripped but for his quick reflexes. He eased me back up. Once standing on my own two feet again, he turned me around with such deliberate strength I was impressed. He laid me against the tiles and dropped to his knees. He licked the water as it trickled down my body.

From the cup of my navel, he drank. The sipping sound he made was so sexy, especially knowing that he was drinking off my body.

I spread my legs and rested fully against the wall. I could feel my legs tense under the weight. I also wanted to enjoy this. He took the opening of my legs as an invitation. He stuck his head there and shoved his tongue in my partly foamy cunt. With his lips, he held my vulva, and then lightly nibbled on it.

I jerked with each nibble. He then licked down and up the lines of my vulva. He was slow and used all of his tongue so I could feel the full weight. Water poured down but he simply redirected that into his mouth and swallowed. At times, he would pump it into my cunt.

When he was done toying with me, he sat me on the edge of the tub and pushed my legs apart. He used his fingers to divide my puzzy in two then licked on my clit. First a lick, then two, then three in rapid succession. Then he would press his mouth against it and grip it firmly before sucking it. He repeated those motions with speed.

He sucked and licked and sucked and licked. I went up and down, up and down. As we rode the fire, he inserted his thumb into my vagina. He wiggled it a bit, removed it and inserted his index finger.

By now, my clits had hardened. It had come out of the fold. The whole pussy tongue was pink and on fire. His licks played games with my nerves while his sucks tripped my mind.

My body went into spasm when he placed one finger in my anus and another two in my nunu. He finger fucked, sucked and slurped me.

Then he stopped, turned me over and inserted his large dick inside me.

The bugger was something. His moves were smooth and strategic. His nut hit all the right spots. So did his fingers he had in my ass. I was suddenly being fucked both ways simultaneously. This was heaven. No one had ever fucked both holes together.

He just stopped, got up and left. I felt him fumble about a bit, as I shouted, "Wheh ley heh you doing? You belleh bring yorseh back here ehn. Ahn like nonsense oh!" My feelings were all over the place and he stopped! "You crackay or wha? I coming kay somebahlay charh nah-nah. Wheh kinnah nonsense dis?" I wondered as I found myself dropping out of the magical zone.

Then he hopped on the bed.

"Ay belleh be..."

I felt the hot oil touch my skin. He began robbing it all over me. It was a scented massage oil- one of those edible brands. He massaged my tata firmly and poured more over the clit.

Unhurriedly, his tongue slid over my lower area before settling on my vulva. He parted it and lightly placed his finger on my puzzy tongue, drew a line around it and inserted the rest under me. He sucked on the oil. He actually sucked as if it was some lollipop. The sucking and smacking sounds exploded my head.

The boy dirty me. I mean, he did not for once, give me a break. If he wasn't under, he was inside some hole. A finger. A didlo. A prick. A finger. A didlo. A prick.

He paused for another moment. By now, I was on to him. I wondered what other dirty trick he was about to play until I felt the coldness on my body. He poured the chocolate syrup spread from my nipples, down to my navel and licked it. He applied a handful all over my vagina, and then he set out to clean it with his tongue. All that fire inside me was quenched by the cold chocolate spread. My last thought was me coming in his mouth as he received my cum, the spread and everything else. He just took them all.

3

Explosive Love

Quickie

"Darling!" he yelled out my name.

"Yes sweetheart!" I replied from in the kitchen. "I will be right there."

I hurried over once I was done with what I was doing. I opened the door but he was not on the bed. A few steps in and still no signs of him.

"Boom! He popped from behind me and grabbed my neck. He kissed it a few times and spun me around.

"What are you do..." I did not finish my question when one hand grabbed my ass and began robbing it. The other, was already under the big t-shirt I wore.

"Hey, I have something on the fi..."

"Shoo," he whispered before kissing my lips hard. He pressed me against the door as it slammed. His finger went straight inside me when my back hit the door.

"Ouch!" I cried, as I was still dry as the Sahara Desert.

"Hmm uhm," he muttered. He was on fire; purely in his animal zone. That shid turns me on. It makes me feel desired. I began to secrete as he moaned, kissed and fingered me.

I reached for his groans. He was fully erected. "Dam," I thought. "I want all of this in me."

He now had my leg raised as he braced it with his free hand. This gave him the space to fist me.

"Oh gal, I want that pussy. Make it wet for me. Please. Make it wet let me fuck you."

His words only fueled my metabolism to pump more juices out of my vagina, just the way he liked it.

Unable to stand it anymore, he turned me around, bent me over and pushed himself deep inside me.

My body trembled. With each thrust, my head lightly banged the door but I couldn't be bothered. I placed my hand on his butt and pinched it in rhyme with his thrusts. He seemed to be enjoying the pain because he humped harder, thus making me to pinch deeper into his skin. He pulled a bunch of my hair lightly, tilting my head up, in a backward slant. I was now positioned at an angle that made it easy for him to enter right into my womb. My head was spinning.

"Oh shit!"

"You like that?"

"Yes baby."

"You want more?"

"Yes."

"Then take it."

"Oh, yes, but slow down baby."

"Gimme that ass."

"Please slow down."

"You said you want it right?"

"Yes! But it hurts."

"I'm coming baby. I'm coming."

With that, his body began violently shaking. He was going full speed; my womb was sweltering, almost exploding. I was wet, burning and just about to climax when I felt him stiffen. I pulled him closer, "You can't fucking stop now. I'll kill you. You better fuck me"

He screamed as he banged away a few more times, then went limp.

By now, I began squirting. My legs were shaking as I held on to the doorknob for support. The world was blurred. The energy in me quickly ran out. I reached for the floor and just lay there, jerking. Moments later, my body went still.

Squeaky

"Hi honey, how is your morning going?"

"Easy, you know. The morning is slow and picking up. Yours?

"It was quite busy but it has settled. It is going to be a tough day, that much I can tell." From his voice, I could tell that he was a bit tense.

"You sound stressed. Is there anything I could do?"

"You could work one of your magical quickies." He giggled. "That is if you were here. You don't worry. I will be fine."

"Yeah, if I was there. How long to your next meeting?"

"About twenty-five minutes."

"Why don't you play some of those relaxing music you love so dearly? Let them calm you down in the absence of my magic touch."

"Nothing substitutes your touch darling- magical or otherwise."

"Awe, so sweet. I'll make this up to you I promise."

"You better. You better gal."

Ten minutes later, his phone rang. "Sir, there's an emergency down in the maintenance room. You are needed here immediately." With that, he cut off the phone.

That was strange. He recognized the voice of the maintenance section head, Zayzay. He was a man of little words. He was also practical. If Zayzay felt he was needed, then he was needed.

He saved his file and hurried downstairs. He entered the common hall and asked the first person he met, "Where is Mr. Zayzay?"

"Over in his office I guess."

The office was one floor above. It was the central room of cubicles overlooking the main floor below. It was partitioned by plywood, a few large windows.

"Knock, knock." He rocked on the door. The noise made it difficult to make out the voice. He repeated his knock. When he still heard nothing, he pushed the door open.

The room was a total mess. Papers were spread out all over the place, tools were stacked everywhere. Against both walls were shelves loaded with every kind of equipment there was and in no particular order. No one was in the swivel chair.

He hesitate briefly but then stepped in the room, leaving the door to swing shut. He looked around and still saw no one. Amidst the stale scented room, a light, sensual smell emitted. He was trying to figure out its source when he felt tender fingers cover his eyes.

He turned in time to see her smile. "What..."

She cut short his question when she reached for his penis through his zipper. It was still lame but not for long. "You..."

"Hush, we nah geh plenty time, you yorseh wor saying aye."

She fell to her knees, put her lips over his dick, and began sucking. He made no attempt to resist.

"ehn you supposed to be at ley conference?" He said as he held her head with both hands.

She kept sucking while fingering herself. "Oh, Hmmm." She moaned. His grip tightened as he got rock hard. She abruptly stood and took two steps toward the shelf on her right.

"No way, you can't stap na ..." He snapped out of his heaven, opened his eyes. She had lifted her skirt and bent over.

He rushed over, pulled her panties aside and pushed his hard dick into her. She was soft and sticky wet.

"Oh!" she moaned.

"Dammit geh, you already wet oh; jeh ley way I like ay."

"Yes darling, I make ay wet for you."

"Yor nah playing oh."

He could not resist the ball of fire rising in him. He banged harder, faster. The shelf she rested her hands on was shaking and squeaking with the rhythm of his thrusts.

"Squeaky, squeaky."

"Yeh baybay."

"Squeaky, squeaky, squeaky...

"Fuck dah pussy boy."

"You won me to fuck dat ass?"

"Yes baybay. Fuck ay like you mean ay"

"Spreh dah ass. Spreh aye honey."

"Aye opin o. I opin aye wah for you."

"Dis is ley fucking best pussy."

"Den take ay nah. Everything for you."

"Yes. Dah ma fucking wet pussy."

"Fastor baby. Fastor."

"Spread ay."

"Okay aye opin."

"I wey fuck kay."

"Yeah nah. Juke ay mehn. Harh"

"I mon fuck kay harh?"

"Yeh, puh ley deep insah. Harder."

"I love dis pussy darling."

"Den fuck me harh nah. Harder. Do wey ruf so I mon come!"

"Yea, jeh fucking come."

"Oh honey, stap fucking playing wey me mehn. Juke dah nut insah ma nunu."

"Squeaky, squeaky, squeaky...

"I'm going to tear it."

"Squeaky, squeaky, squeaky," squeaked the shelf.

"Tear ay! Fucking rip it."

"You won me to teah ay, den opin lah womb. I wey show you who be who."

"Squeaky, squeaky, squeaky...

"Fasterrrr. Deep-eeer. F-u-c-k. Fu-ck. Fuck. Fuck. Fuck. Fuck. I coming!"

"Squeaky, squeaky, squeaky...

"Yes. Come. Come. Come. Baby."

"I coming mehn. Aye coming baby. Juke ay harh mehn. Leh me fucking come."

"Yes come. Make dat pussy wet. Come wey me nah. Leh come together baby."

"Squeaky, squeaky, squeaky..." the shelf sounded even louder.

"Oh yes! Oh, yes! Yes! Yes! Yes!"

"I coming oh!"

"Me too! I coming! I coming! I coming! I fucking c-o-m-i-n-g!"

She trembled. Her legs shook violently. Even the shelf vibrated. For a moment there, he feared it would come crumbling down as he exploded!

4

The Experiments

Going All Out

I had been fucking Kromah, my husband's best friend, on and off, for the last six months. Why? I don't know. I have known him for all ten years of my marriage. He was the best man at our wedding. I never thought of him as anything more than a family friend. Not until the day, he came over to help me with my car.

My husband had left town for business. I had a flat tire on my way from work, so I reached out to him for help. It was scolding hot. I was on my second bottle of water when he finally showed up. I was hot and annoyed.

"You look hot," he said.

Irritated, I replied, "I am hot".

He replied with a quick, "I know". It sounded different; it sounded more like a compliment than an agreement. He had walk over to the trunk of my car to get my spare tire.

"What do you mean, 'you know'?" I asked.

"I know you are hot."

He turned and looked at me, his eyes undressing me. You could tell he was having dirty thoughts. I didn't want to pay any mind to it, so I brushed it off as a weak attempt at humor or flirting.

He continued speaking as he walked towards me, "I know you are hot, that's why I go to bed every night thinking about you and my dick inside you." By this time, he was up close. I could smell the mixture of cane juice and kola nut on his breath.

Then I saw it. His penis had erected. I was stunned. I didn't know what to do.

Anything Goes? Anything Doesn't Go

He firmly took my hand and placed it on his dick. My heart leaped. I'm not sure what the leap was for, fear, shock or excitement. I have not had a dick that size in ten years. It was strong, hard, damn right commanding.

His muscles were popping from under the tight black t-shirt he was wearing. His sweaty scent made me so damn horny.

He put his arms around me and grabbed on my lips with his teeth. I hesitantly put my arms around his neck and pull him closer.

He took the gesture as acceptance. With one swift motion, he used both of his arms and shoved me down to the ground. Not too hard though. I dropped to my knees, my eyes level to his bursting pants. He unzipped his jeans, pulled out his dick and shoved it into my mouth.

The screaming sound from the car flying by, "Get a damn room," was what reminded me that I was on the highway. At that moment, I didn't care who was watching. Matter of fact, the thought of someone watching had my pussy overflowing with juice.

By now, his long and hard dick was pulsating every few seconds. I grabbed it, stuck in in my mouth and sucked it with all of my heart. He moaned. I sucked harder.

Then, he bended me over the hood of the car, and thrusted his dick deep inside me.

Immediately, I felt it hit my G-spot so I leapt from under him. He pull me back and bend me over, this time in a position that had my body locked under him. He was hungry for my pussy. His dick was moving 80mph inside me.

"This nut is too dam big!" I felt it rip against my pussy walls. I couldn't stand it. I needed to move. I was struggling to breathe, my legs was giving up. I felt it shaking. Even the car's hood couldn't hold me up much longer. My fingers were losing their grip. I was certain that I was about to fainted.

"Get out!" I barked.

"Not yet."

No, I can't take it anymore. It is hurting me."

"So what must I do with it now?"

I don't care, just take that shit out of my womb. You are spoiling it. Take it out now, please.

"Then open your mouth. You want it in your mouth."

"Just take it out. I'll take it anywhere else but in my pussy."

Just like that, without warning, he stopped. I fell to the floor, on my knees, before I realized he had stopped. I was dizzy. I felt my head turning as he held it upright and shoved his monster dick in my mouth. I fought to get it out but his hands were firmly holding both sides of my head around my temples.

He fucked my mouth as hard as he had my pussy. I could barely take all of him inside. I felt him hitting the back of my throat. I gagged and choked. The saliva kept dropping as he slurped in and out of my mouth.

Suddenly without warning, I felt a hot, sour moistness in my mouth. I had swallowed some before I realized that he had put his sperm in my mouth, deep down right into my throat. I could not believe it. I felt the tension of his fingers release as he ever so gently let go of my head. I was just glad to finally be able to breathe some fresh air.

I started coughing immediately. I fell to the floor, hands and knees. I spat out what was left. As I collected myself, I could not stop thinking how this was the first time I had swallowed cum— something I hadn't done ever before, not even for my husband. It didn't taste like I had imagined.

I sat on the ground and lain against the car. My tata was breathing, so was my mouth. I was burning. My whole body was hot and sweaty. I felt nasty but dam good too.

After a while, I strangely started getting horning for more of that dick. "Oh lawd no! I must stop before he tears my pussy or burst my womb. I wanted it but couldn't handle it.

5

Re-Capturing My Soul

Discovering Me

I was lost. At least I felt so. I could not feel anything; okay not anything. I felt pain in one place. I had just woken up feeling all nasty about myself. My ass hurt me as if it was on fire. I mean each breath I draw, sends pain down there. I dread having to move. I may just lay my ass down in this bed all day.

"What the fuck happened last night?" I wondered. Vague memories pop in and out of my already pounding head.

There was noise, plenty drinking and yelling. Then some weed and tramadol. "Did I take some?"

"Hell no," the softer voice in my head retorted. Good, because I know I don't take that shit. I stay far away from drugs of any kind. That ain't life. It is the quickest way to die.

"So, if I didn't take it, why do I feel like shit?" My mind kept throwing these questions back at me. I hated it when I had to deal with shids and it did that bookish shit to me. I can't think far today, I can't.

Outside, the city noise hummed beneath. "What was happening to me?"

Then the door opened with a bang. The loudness along with the daylight assaulted me. I covered my face but the sudden movement worsen things. "Shit! Who the hell is that?"

His face appeared in the middle of the hallow then the light vanished.

"Sorry," was all he offered. He'd closed the door with his foot resulting in another bang.

"Ouch."

"Dammit, are you trying to kill me or something?"

"Sorry dear. And no, I'm not trying to kill you. I am actually the one trying to save you. Now you get up and take this medicine. You will feel a lot better when you do."

"Who are you again?"

"Your savoir. Away with the questions. Come take the meds. Even like this, you're still cranky."

I didn't have the strength to argue. I would sell an arm to feel better. I struggle up but he reached out to help steady me. He sat me down and propped pillows against my back. He popped some pills in my hand and I just swallowed the tiny dam shits, not knowing nor caring what they were.

Let's face it. If he'd wanted me drugged, what could I do to stop him? I could not get any more drugged out than I already was. At least I'm risking feeling better with whatever I just took.

Much later, I feel like heaven as compared to earlier. I begin to remember more things. We had had a party here last night. We had drank and done other partyish things too. I recall almost stripping down after too many tequilas and the temptation of winning some money- a lot of money too. I don't recall how we could win, but it was some competition or something and I wanted to win so badly, I went all out. Besides, I needed some extra money.

"You are alright?"

I startled out of my thoughts. "Dam! You got to stop doing that."

"Doing what?"

"Startling me."

"Oh that."

"Yes, that."

For the first time, I looked across from me and recognized him. He was the cool dude I was crushing. He is reserved and keeps to himself in the office. Unlike the other guys, he never goes out of his way to show how big a pair of balls he has. He is gentle and respectful. He speaks to everyone and stays to himself as much as he can. He is not a loner though, just private.

I like that about him. Privacy. I price mine above most things. Anyone who shares this quality, has good marks in my book. But how I ended up here with him, remains foggy.

"Can I ask you something?"

"Sure. Anything."

"Did we..."

He laughed loudly. That made me feel stupid. Then he calmed down and stared at me. "What do you think? You're here in my house, on my sofa, naked. So tell me. What do you think happened." He offered that crooked smile that says, "I am totally messing with you." Then he got serious. "You truly don't remember right?"

"No, I don't." I bent my head down shamefully.

He reached out his hand and carefully took mine. "We left the party sober but you insisted I take you anywhere else but home. We hopped around a bit then came here. We drank too much and made out."

"Is that all?"

"Basically."

"Basically?"

"Yeah."

"What is that to mean?"

"Nothing. Why do you have to read something into it?"

"Why are you being evasive?" I had the feeling he was leaving something out.

"Well, you want the details of the sex too? If you don't remember then surely it wasn't superb."

After a long, uncomfortable pause, he leaned forward. He sat in the opposite chair. "How do I say this?"

"Raw. Simple."

"We had sex."

"Isnt that obvious by now?"

"And it was ... okay."

"Okay? I never do okay sex. Now I got you. I knew you were holding back. What are you not telling me? Spill it out. I am grown enough."

"It was rough."

"A bit too rough?"

"Yeah."

"How 'a bit' is a bit?"

"Nine, on a scale of four."

"Hmm. Okay, so I fucked you twice over, why are you jittery? You surely have been fucked many times. This can't be your first good fuck. Or, are you a virgin, a mumu or a boy?

"Let's say, I am, so what?"

"You're lying. If you won't say what happened, then I better go." I got up to go only to realize that I was truly nude as he had mentioned before. Shit. I reached for my breasts, then on second thought, removed my hands and slowly looked around for my clothes. If he were going to toy with me, I would do same. I took my time 'checking'. When I found nothing in the sofa, I squatted right in front of it. Then I bent over, exposing my pussy and butt for him to see. I felt him fidget a bit.

I drop into the sofa and bent over its back as if I was looking for something behind it. I lifted one foot over and searched on the right side arm area.

"Fuck," he got up, if it is your clothes you want, they are messed up. You may have to wear a shit of mine and any pant that fits you."

"Messed up? How?"

"With things."

I liked how this made him uncomfortable. So, I turned around and slumped back in the chair. This time, I left my legs apart. I saw him steal glances right inside my pussy-hole. I just sat there with my head leaned over the backrest. Whatever he was doing, I paid no mind.

Before I knew it, he was on top of me. He pushed my legs wider and put his head there. As his mouth touched my pussy, I jerked. Everything down there felt sore. But the sensation was also sweet, so I settled down, relaxed my body and I let him go on. I was curious to know his skills. I was not going to walk out of here forgetting a whole night.

He slurped his tongue over my nunu professionally. "Dam, he was good." I moaned each time his wet tongue passed over my clit area.

He pulled apart my labia majora and licked my clits. A shock went up my vertebra. He paused then held it in place and sucked that clitoris. He sucked, then licked, then wiggle his tongue. He repeated this rhythm sending me into a violent rage.

"Oh suck me! Fucking suck that pussy."

"Hmmm nddd hhmm lasjd!"

I didn't understand shit he was trying to ay. I just wanted him to keep his mouth occupied in my nunu. For all I cared, nothing he needed to say now mattered. He should just keep his dam head between my legs, sucking my life out.

He abruptly got up and lifted me, turned me around and started fucking me doggy style. As he entered, my entire fish felt sore. My ass too. It was painful. It felt as if he had placed a rod in my fish.

"You want me to fist you like last night?"

"Fist me?" I thought. "Hell no, I ain't want no fisting."

It is as if he read my mind, but he instead fingered my butt. Putting those fingers in my ass sent pain straight to my head. I screamed. But he was too fast. He already was thrusting in and out before I could figure out what was happening. I had only one thought. "How did my ass get that free to allow him in like that?"

Next thing I knew, he was fucking me there. His cock was wet with saliva and it went right in. now that was alarming. "What the fuck was happening here?" surprisingly, before I could voice that out, I felt something in my whole body. The dude had hit my G-spot right on. It was electric. The sensation was different. It took over the nerves and rode the waves deliberately, then violently. The shid was magical.

Only once before, had I ever felt anything near this. And that was after much reading and exploration- looking for the fucking G-spot. I assumed it was. I would never have suspected it was in my ass.

I didn't want him to stop. I was coming and it felt amazing. I didn't just jerk but I convulsed with each stroke. The deeper, the better it felt. He needed to do this endlessly. I wasn't warm, this orgasm was loaded, it felt heavy. It was activated my mind in ways unknown. I was hot but not on fire.

By the time he finished, I had come three times already. I didn't even notice him stiffen and jerk the way men do when they are coming. I only noticed when he went limp inside me.

"Why the fuck are you stopping?"

"I came."

"Just like that? I want more!"

"Well let me rest. You are insatiable. I never would have suspected."

"Does that bother you?"

"Not at all. I actually like a woman who is bold about her sexuality."

We rested a bit with me rested in his arms as he fondled my hair. "Can I ask you something?"

"Sure you can."

"What really happened last night?" Honestly, tell me please."

"Hmm." He clear his throat.

I looked up at him with expectancy. I had a feeling about this. What exactly I felt, I can't tell, I just felt some way.

"We had wild sex last night. I did things I had never done before and I suspect neither have you. You insisted, so I obliged. I swear, I didn't feel like you were taken advantage of; if I had, I would have stopped. I just feel you might regret afterwards. I don't know why I feel that way."

"Was it bad? I mean the 'things'? Kinky?"

"Kinky as fuck."

"Okay."

"No not okay. You ere wild, you asked me to fist you. I had to use all my fingers, and still you wanted more. It was a bit uncomfortable for me at first, but I saw how you enjoyed it so I figured you out for one of those freak kinds."

"Oh that will explain the easy access."

"Access?"

"Never mind. Then what else?"

"You didn't just stop there, you wanted, deep, raw anal too. I had to be rough or you'd kill me. At least according to you."

"So, did you do it?"

"What?"

"Oh, yeah. I believe you said you came each of the three times we did it. I was particularly concerned with the fisting and object parts."

"Wait a minute. You mean...?"

"Yes."

"And ...?"

"Yes. You were something else. Youre as fetish as fuck. I swear gal. You and all the squirting. I am surprised I would never have figured you out for one."

I sat pondering. He just looked at me. No judgement, no justification needed. He simply looked. That was good. I would hate to be under the microscope now. He figured I didn't need that.

"I am glad you told me. I would not have believed you if I hadn't experienced it all just now, nor had I not felt the sore I feel now. Even now, I am surprised at how much I enjoyed it.

No Regrets

Mamasie is my brother's jue. She's dam hot with round, full breast that bounce with the slightest motion. She doesn't always wear bra around the house. He ass is curved in all the right places- sidepiece and backside.

It is one of those watery, moochy, asses, that will follow its owner left, right, then up and down. When she moves, it moves. She takes time walking around. Trust me, you don't want to experience it when you're horny. The girl is a tsunami of fresh, full, Lorma ass.

Lately, they have been fussing a lot. He goes out all day, comes home late and has enough energy only to eat and boss her around. She being a loyal wife, doesn't have much of a choice.

When our parents arranged their marriage, both were little. Even as they grew up, they never seemed to have connected.

She liked things he didn't like. She loved ground pea soup he hated it. She was quiet and he was loud. She preferred to be alone while he wanted

Gurley Street Love

people all around. She was fundamentally different from him. I think I can safely say they hated each other.

Our Ma, had noticed and tried to talk our Pa out of it. She had suggested that I marry her since we seemed to be a better fit. But my father said no. he believed in time, they would get over it.

The truth is, he didn't care. The marriage was strategic. Father wanted one of his boys married into the Bah family. It was that simple. The rest of his reasons, we never knew and might never find out.

Of late, I noticed her crying and sniffing whenever she was alone. So, I took upon myself to check on her. You know, the usual popping in and asking if

93

she is fine and wither I could help with anything or in anyway. I simply wanted to keep her happy.

One day, I knocked on the door and was sure I heard an answer. So, I pushed the door and entered. There she was, on the bed, with one leg raised as she creamed. Naked. I froze looking at her fat, shaved puzzy all spread open like that.

My nut kicked straight up. It fought to free itself from in the jeans trousers I wore. It throbbed up and down in a pausing motion. She startled and stopped moving. In that brief moment, nothing obstructed my view into her nunu. It was bushy but it was hard to miss the pink lips in that dark forest.

Eventually, I managed to find my voice, apologized and backed out, with my hard dick still fighting for first place. I went directly to the bathroom and masturbated. I knew of no other way to ease that stress. With every stroke, I imagined her spread open for me. It didn't take long for me to come.

The rest of the day, we stole glances at each other. It didn't feel uncomfortable, just okay. No one spoke a word to the other but the tension was there.

The next day, around the same time, I braved going into the room. This time, She didn't startle. She sat expectantly. When she finished creaming, she stood, slowly and walked to the dressing mirror to complete her dressing. After she wore her hijab, I left the room. We danced this music for few more days but never acted upon it. Each day, I saw more of her.

A week into our routine, I decided to be bold. As soon as I entered the room, I went straight to her and grabbed her ass. I parted it and shoved my erected cock into her pussy. Surprisingly, she was wet. It was tight, fleshy and warm.

We didn't have time, my mother was outside somewhere and could walk in at any time. We were taking huge risks here. This was my big brother's wife.

I heard her struggle to hold her scream inside as I forced my long dick inside of her. I pulled out and went right back in. my thrusts were hard, direct and fast. In-out, in-out. Soon, she began to move with my rhythm. I fucked her so hard, that by the time I came, I felt my nut squeezed.

For the next six months, we fucked every chance we got. We fucked everywhere we could manage. Sometimes, in the kitchen, behind the door, in the children's room. One time, we even fucked right in the hallway.

Each time, it was the same. Quick. Fast. Hard and dirty. We never had time for foreplay or anything. She didn't wear panties often, so it was just the matter of lifting her lappa, skirt or dress. I didn't wear briefs much either. I simply lifted my robe, twisted my boxers, if I happened to wear one, and in I would go. Sometimes, she was wet and other times, she was dry as fuck. Those were the times that my nut would hurt me the whole day. I would feel it rip away at the walls of her vagina. I could tell how painful it was, but there was not much I could do, but put saliva on it, and go right back in. Her pussy was so tight, it made me to come in no time.

One day, as we were fucking in the room, my mother barged in. had she not stopped to attend to my little brother who had come crying to her at the door, she would have walked in on a sight. I had her bent over doggy style. I was humping away.

I rushed under the bed and stayed there for almost twenty minutes. When our ma left, I rushed out from under the bed and finished off what we had started. This particular fuck was so sweet. I didn't want it to stop.

There was this one time she was cooking in the kitchen. We didn't get chance in the room. In fact, recently, it was so difficult to get her alone. We had some guests. When they left, my mother started spending more time with Mamasie.

So, when Mama left us to take her bath. We jumped on it. I pushed her behind the door, bent her to her knees and put my dick in. I was so much in a hurry and stealing glances around, I mistakenly put my nut in her ass. She screamed a little but covered her mouth in time. I quickly dipped my hand in the oil, rubbed it and went right back in. I fucked her until I came.

We had the best sex everywhere we could for the next six months. One morning, I snuck in to find her vomiting in the bathroom.

Months later, she gave my brother a son- our son. For months, we had nothing to do. My life was boring, but last evening, I cornered her in the other room and fingered her good. She even allowed me to come in her hand. Then she said, "Soon, we'd start again. Soon."

I look forward to fucking Mamasie, my brother's wife. I wish I could marry her but...

6

Revamping Our Groove

Bitchy Payback

Lately, sex has been mechanical. Nothing has been magical about it. He rolls over me, makes a few lazy thrusts, comes and falls asleep. Or I hop on him, ride him for some time and then come. I just roll back down and we fall asleep. I make no fuss because I equally share the blame.

The work has piled up on me. The weekly shows and the biweekly community engagement are in full swing. The community of writers has upped their game. More things are in play. Often, by the time I get home, nothing is more precious than the bed. Sometimes, I'm too exhausted to even take a bath. I have time only for late supper in bed. If I am lucky, I'd wash my vagina and wipe it after my bathroom rounds.

When Vamba joins me, he is equally tired. His rounds are not any different from mine. He isn't any less busy than I am but we try to keep the flame alive. At least we think so.

Despite our efforts, we were unsuccessful. The mechanical sex is just enough to KO both of us. We keep promising to do it better.

Last night though, it was different. When he entered me, he was not as hard as he should be but was harder than lately. He even displayed some of his energy and machoism I miss from the sex machine I know he was.

He was on his knees, fucking me. I was turned on my left side, giving him a twisted angle into my vagina. He was hitting the right spot. Midway through his thrusts, he called her name.

I froze. Every sensation left me. I turned sideways to see his face but he was oblivious to it. I was irritated as fuck. I wanted to push him away but the other part of my brain was unable to do anything.

"How dare him?" Fucking her behind me isn't enough he has to utter her name while at it?" I felt abused and angry. He had betrayed my trust and worse, insulted me without even being aware of it.

This bothered me for some time as I withdrew. My mood was often cool or cold. I could not bring myself to sleeping with him after that. It took him a while to notice but he finally did.

In my struggle, he didn't seem to care. He asked and tried to get me into my mojo but it never happened. I could not bring myself to that point.

After much contemplation, I decided to repay him. I fixed him some nice dinner, his favorite cassava leaf. Then I waited for him.

As he entered, I rushed to him, kissed him and pushed him against the wall. I unzipped his pants, took his crumpled nut, and put it in my mouth. I sucked on it while rubbing his balls. In no time, he was hard as fuck. Like Jomah, my ex, he loved my head, I knew he did so I gave him what he wanted. When he was as hard as I wanted, I shoved it in me.

I was still dry but I wanted him hard, dry and fucking rough. I was not going to miss my action. Of that, I was certain.

He was so into his mojo and began taking control of the sex. He flipped me around and put me on my knees. He forced his way in me and fucked me hard.

As he was enjoying, I moaned, "Fuck me hard!"

"Yes baby, I will tear that puzzy!"

"Yes, tear it."

"Then open it wide."

"It is all yours."

"Yes, it is mine. Say it!"

"It is yours, baby."

"Louder!"

"Oh yes, it is all fucking yours."

"You like it?"

"Yesssss!" I was close to coming so the rhythm increased.

"You want it?"

"Yes I do. Fuck it." Vamba rammed so hard, my tata was crying, even my waist was in pain from his grip.

"Whose puzzy is this?"

"Yours."

"Say it louder geh!"

"Y-o-u-r-s baaaaby!" I yelled.

"Say my fucking name woman."

"Oh yes baby, do it, it's coming. Do it fast. Hard. Fast."

My legs shook. My body exploded and I began jerking.

Like a maniac out of control, he fucked and slapped me while yelling, "Whose cunt is this!"

"It's yours."

"Yes, say who owns it."

"You."

"Say the name gal.!"

As I hit my orgasm, I screamed, "Yours, Jooo-mahhhh!"

7

Freedom

Slave No More

I'm sitting here in the bathroom, on the toilet, crying my eyes out. My inside is sore; I have bruises all over my body from a weekend of thrust and rough sex. "Why? Why? Why did he have to be so cruel to my vagina?"

I begged for mercy, but he didn't let off. Maybe he was confused by the mixed messages I sent, "Please stop, please stop. No don't stop. Okay stop, pleasssse! Oh my god, don't stop, don't stop." It was a merciless, fuck feast. I don't know what was I thinking.

I am an emotional mess. I can't keep a man, no matter how hard they try, to keep me, I find every reason in the world to boot them out of my life.

I was driving up country to my little spot in the woods, to calm down from a hectic week. The ideal of being alone in my cabinet was so entertaining, until I came across the sexist hitch-hacker I have ever seen.

He was bald headed, his body was drained in sweat, and the darkness of his skin was shining, bright, in the sun, I just couldn't resist. I pulled over. He ran up to the car.

"Big sis, can I get a ride?"

"It depends. Where are you going?"

"As far as you are willing to take me. I'm just trying to leave my village and go make life somewhere. Anywhere, but here."

"Hmm. Get in."

He jumped in so fast it scared me shitless. What if he is a society man? Or what if he rapes me. My mind began playing some games on me. I had to remind myself that it was okay and he was none if those horrible things.

Then, the thought hit me. "Hmm, I could pay him to do to me whatever I wish."

"So, how are you planning on making life? Do you have any skills or work experience?"

"Not really, but I am good with my hands."

"Would you like to make some money tonight?"

"Tonight?"

"Yes. Tonight."

"Doing what?"

"Doing whatever I tell you to."

"I don't mind, so long it doesn't require me breaking the law."

"You won't be breaking the law. When we get to my village. You just take a hot shower, and follow my instructions."

He looked at me and smiled. By this time, he had gotten the picture and it seems like he was down for whatever.

There was something erotic and dangerous about him. I could see it in his eyes, and the question "what if" turned me the fuck on.

We pulled up into my yard. Even though, the hut was made out of mud, it contained some of the nicest furniture and gadgets of our time. It was set apart from the other huts for privacy. I wanted to be *here* but not *here*. I wanted to be away from the stress but comfortable in the solitude.

I directed him to the bathroom. There was a huge drum of water in there. He made himself comfortable with a quick bath. When he came out, in just a tower wrapped around his waist, my heart cut.

I could trace clear lines from his biceps to many other parts of his body. The muscles were firm and strong. The beads of water over his dark skin sent me loco. My vagina lost control of its fluid.

I hurriedly undressed and rushed into the bathroom for a shower but not before seeing his snake shaking under the tower he wore. It was breathing in response to my nakedness.

Few minutes later, when I walked back into the bedroom, he was laying on the bed, back down, penis upright and ready for my command. It was everything I envisioned, tip red, long, thick and hard.

My oversized breasts dangled with the nipples hard as rock. My unshaved pubic hair was rough and spread all over.

"Come sit on it," he said with a smile.

"I thought I was the one giving the commands here? I guess you must have been confused. I command, you obey."

"Okay, what is your command?" he asked.

On second thoughts, I pondered, "I had given commands all week to my staff; I didn't mind taking it from the sexy guy on my bed." So, I walked over and sat right on it. Of course, it went right in because my puzzy was already as wet as freaking duck just from a pond.

He fastened my arms behind my back and flipped me over. Strength, yes strength, he embodies strength. His hands firmly gripped my neck. He tightened his hand and whispered in my ear, "Is this what you want?"

"Hmm-uhm." Words struggled to make their way out of my mouth.

His other hand slowly made its way down my belly. Then, with a firm gentleness, he slide his fingers into my puzzy. The whole thing happened as if in slow motion.

Once in, he tightened his grip harder around my neck, I couldn't breathe. "You're so fucking wet right now," he said, his fingers going deeper and faster inside me. He finger fucked me for a while before removing his hand from under me. He placed it in his mouth and licked my juices off it. Abruptly, he put the same fingers in my mouth. I sucked on it, tasting a sweat mixture of pussy, saliva and mucus. At the same time, I felt him push his dick inside of me.

The boy was something else. He fucked me hard, he fucked me deep, and fucked me rough for one straight hour no stop. Thre-quarters of an hour in, I realized I had come at least four times- that is way more than I had ever come in one straight fuck. Each time I came, I jerked violently and he rammed me harder and crazier than ever.

By the end of the hour mark, I was about to come again, when I felt him stiffen, then pause, only to pick up his tempo. I swear I felt his nut way in my stomach, just past my womb. That is how deep he went when he was about to come. Still choking lightly and squeezing he came like a river inside me,. I exploded with a cunt full of squirt that rolled all down his dick.

By the end of it, I was so beat up, I didn't realized he'd left. He returned a bit later, woke me and placed before me a whole meal.

As I sit over this toilet, trying to ease my pain, I'm also considering the ideal of keeping him around a little longer.

Epilogue

"Hhmm," I just fucking loved his cock. It felt like a rod inside my pussy; and when he pounded, I could feel it inside my womb. Hard, steady strokes just at the right places. He was brutish. He knew he was hurting me but it seemed that's exactly what he wanted. I wanted it to stop, but then again, I didn't.

"Dam," this pussy is sweet. It is tight with walls I can feel pressing against my dick as I go in and out. It is dry enough to feel a scrape with each insertion. "Mehn, dah dis kina puzzy dah you keep. You can't mess wey aye."

They fucked for the next hour plus before either felt like taking a rest. He rolled over and fell straight asleep, exhausted. She just kept laying halfway on the bed and half on the floor. She was too tired to move.

They stayed that way for the longest time, until he woke up and suddenly started eating her puzzy. He took it in his mouth and let his tongue wiggle away, giving her the utmost orgasm.

About the Authors

D. Othniel Forte is the author of over ten books of fiction and nonfiction.

He is the editor of KWEE, Liberian Literary Magazine and a publisher.

Berenice A. Mulubah authored *Landing Safely On A Solid Rock,* and *Honey Purple Lips*. A poet, singer, blogger and designer. She served in the United States Marine Corps, and was a contractor with the FBI.

A Liberian native, she is a lover of arts and culture, currently residing in North Carolina.

Other Books In the series

Vagina Rules

Coming Soon.

Puzzy Diary

Pleasure Principles

Vagina Reigns

Penis Code